Is Anybody Up?

written and illustrated by **Ellen Kandoian**

G. P. Putnam's Sons
New York

Copyright © 1989 by Ellen Kandoian
All rights reserved. Published simultaneously in Canada.
Printed in Hong Kong by South China Printing Co.
Library of Congress Cataloging-in-Publication Data
Kandoian, Ellen. Is anybody up? / written and
illustrated by Ellen Kandoian. p.   cm.
Summary: Although Molly in the United States is far away
from the Inuit woman of Baffin Bay and the lonely sailor off the
coast of Chile, they all eat breakfast at the same time because
they are in the same time zone.
ISBN 0-399-21749-5
[1. Longitude – Fiction. 2. Manners and customs – Fiction.
3. Breakfasts – Fiction.]   I. Title.
PZ7.K1274Is   1989 [E] – dc19 88-38098 CIP AC

First Impression

*In loving memory
of Arpen,
my grandmother*

1888–1986

Sometimes when Molly wakes up and goes downstairs, the house is very quiet. She wonders, is anybody up?

Even if she is the first one up on Saturday morning
and makes her own breakfast, Molly has lots of company.

Far to the north and far to the south, it is seven-thirty
in the morning and other people are getting up
and having breakfast too.

To the north, on Baffin Bay, an Inuit woman is making griddle cakes and tea for breakfast.

In Quebec, a boy is fixing French toast.

A cat in New York City is having some milk for breakfast.

To the south, in Miami, Molly's grandfather
is making scrambled eggs and coffee.

In Haiti, a little girl is eating peanut butter on bread and a banana for breakfast.

A great parrot in Colombia is nibbling some mangoes.

High in the Andes of Peru, a little boy is eating roasted corn for breakfast.

Down in the southern Pacific Ocean, off the coast of Chile, a lonely sailor is having a can of sardines.

And farther south, near Antarctica, a seal is swimming around looking for some fish for breakfast.

Before long, in all these places it will be eight o'clock in the morning. And if someone comes along to share breakfast, it will be time to say —

"Ai!"

"Bonjour!"

"Meow!"

"Good morning!"

"Bonjour!"

"¡Buenos días!"

"Alli llanchu!"

"Ahoy there!"

WAKING UP WITH MOLLY

Although they live in different places, speak different languages, and eat different foods, the people and animals in this story have some important things in common. One is that they all live in the same time zone. For all of them, eight o'clock in the morning comes at the same time.

This isn't true for everyone in the world. The Earth is round, like a ball, so the sun can't shine on everyone everywhere at once. What time of day it is depends on where you live. That is why time zones were invented. The Earth is divided into many time zones, regions stretching from the North Pole to the South Pole, a little like the sections on a beach ball, an orange or a pumpkin. As the Earth turns slowly each day, the sun shines on the different time zones in turn.

Each time zone has a name. We call Molly's the Eastern Time Zone. All around the Earth there are 24 different time zones, one for each hour in the day.